W9-DFA-921

DATE DUE

HEROES OF AMERICAN HISTORY

John F. Kennedy

The 35th President

Carin T. Ford

Enslow Elementary
an imprint of

Enslow Publishers, Inc.

40 Industrial Road	PO Box 38
Box 398	Aldershot
Berkeley Heights, NJ 07922	Hants GU12 6BP
USA	UK

http://www.enslow.com

Enslow Elementary, an imprint of Enslow Publishers, Inc.

Enslow Elementary® is a registered trademark of Enslow Publishers, Inc.

Library of Congress Cataloging-in-Publication Data

Ford, Carin T.
    John F. Kennedy: the 35th president / Carin T. Ford.— 1st ed.
      p. cm. — (Heroes of American history)
    Includes index.
    ISBN 0-7660-2601-9 (hardcover)
    1. Kennedy, John F. (John Fitzgerald), 1917–1963—Juvenile literature. 2. Presidents—United States—Biography—Juvenile literature. I. Title. II. Series.
    E842.Z9F67 2006
    973.922'092—dc22

                                               2005009499

Printed in the United States of America

10 9 8 7 6 5 4 3 2 1

Table of Contents

Eight of the nine Kennedy children,
from youngest to oldest: Jean, Robert, Patricia,
Eunice, Kathleen, Rosemary, Jack, and Joe Jr.

Chapter 1

A Different Kind of Kennedy

Young John F. Kennedy—called Jack—lined up next to his brothers and sisters. It was time for their mother, Rose, to check everyone. Each day, she made sure the children had no spots on their clothes, no buttons missing, no shoelaces untied.

The Kennedys were a rich and famous family. Jack's father was an important businessman. Jack's grandfather was the mayor of Boston. All the Kennedy children were supposed to be well dressed. They also had to be on time for meals, good at sports, and smart in school. "We want winners," Jack's father always said.

But Jack was different from his brothers and sisters. He was sloppy and late. He was always getting sick. So Jack made jokes to get by. He learned to laugh at his troubles. No one dreamed that Jack would grow up to be the most famous Kennedy of them all.

Jack, age six months.

Jack was born on May 29, 1917, in Brookline, Massachusetts. He was the second oldest of Rose and Joseph Kennedy's nine children. Joseph Kennedy was a powerful man. He hoped that one day his eldest son, Joe, would become president of the United States.

Joe was outgoing and athletic, and he did well in school. Jack, on the other hand, often missed school for months at a time because he came down with so many sicknesses. Yet Jack never complained. He read adventure stories in bed, such as *Treasure Island* and *King Arthur and the Knights of the Round Table*.

At fourteen, Jack went to Choate, a boarding school in Connecticut. He was not a good student. Many times, he forgot to bring his books and his

Jack, age five.

pencils to class. Jack kept getting sick, and he grew so thin that his friends called him Rat Face.

Still, Jack liked having fun. He threw oranges out the windows at his friends, and he filled a boy's room with pillows. Once, he stole a cardboard cutout of an actress from a movie theater. Then he put it into his bed to surprise the cleaning woman in the morning. He even started a club for boys who liked playing pranks. After that, Jack was almost kicked out of school.

Jack and his older brother, Joe.

"Rules bother him a bit," said one school official.

Yet in spite of all the trouble Jack caused, everyone liked him.

Chapter 2

College Days

When Jack was nineteen, he went to Harvard University. He made many friends there. He was funny and easy to get along with.

Jack tried out for the swim team and surprised everyone by beating one of Harvard's best swimmers. He also enjoyed writing articles for the school paper, the *Harvard Crimson*. Jack said he had "never been so busy in my whole life."

Jack, far right, with his dad and his brother Joe. All three went to Harvard.

In the spring of 1939, Jack took a break from college and traveled to Europe. A few years earlier, Adolf Hitler had become the leader of Germany. He had attacked Austria and planned to invade other countries. When Jack got back to college, he wrote a long report about what was happening in Europe. The report was published as a book called *Why England Slept*. It became a bestseller.

Jack graduated from college with honors in 1940. By this time, Hitler had attacked many countries, including France and England. The war that was spreading across Europe would become known as World War II.

When Jack was twenty-four years old, he joined the navy. In December 1941, the United States began sending soldiers to fight in World War II, and Jack wanted to fight. The next year, he was sent to the

Jack was becoming very interested in world events.

South Pacific Ocean. Jack took command of torpedo boat PT-109. He was about to become a war hero.

Chapter 3

Taking Charge

Jack and his crew were on board PT-109 one summer night in 1943. A Japanese warship came out of the darkness and rammed Jack's boat—slicing it in half. Two men were killed. Another man, Pat McMahon, was badly burned.

Jack and his crew clung to the pieces of their boat all night long. Finally, Jack ordered everyone to swim to a nearby island. Pat was too hurt to swim. So Jack pulled him along by holding the straps of Pat's life jacket in his teeth. It took five hours of swimming to reach the island. Jack and his crew were finally rescued after a few days. Jack was given medals for his courage and his leadership.

PT-109 was sent to the South Pacific Ocean near the Solomon Islands.

The boat accident had hurt Jack's back. Then he came down with malaria, a sickness that causes fever and chills. Jack was sent back to the United States to get well.

Jack's brother Joe was also fighting in World War II. He was a navy pilot. In August 1944, Joe took off on a secret bombing mission. Something went wrong, and Joe's plane exploded. He was killed instantly. The Kennedy family was heartbroken.

Jack began working as a newspaper reporter. But his father had other ideas. "My father wanted his eldest son in politics," Jack said. "'Wanted' isn't the right word. He demanded it." After Joe's death, Jack was the eldest son.

So in 1946 Jack ran for Congress—the lawmaking part of the government. Jack's brothers and sisters traveled all over the state of Massachusetts, asking people to vote for Jack. He won the election.

At this time, doctors found out that Jack had Addison's disease.

This is one of the last photos taken of Jack, left, with Joe.

Jack told voters that he would be a good congressman.

This illness made it hard for Jack's body to fight infections. It explained why he was sick so often. Jack was given medicine to help the problem. The Kennedys did not tell anyone about Jack's disease. It was a family secret.

Jack was a United States congressman for six years. In 1953, when he was thirty-five, he was elected to the Senate. Jack served as a senator for eight years. The next step would be the White House.

Chapter 4

President Kennedy

Jack had dated many women over the years. Then he met Jacqueline ("Jackie") Bouvier, a newspaper photographer. Jackie came from a wealthy family. She was smart, pretty, and talented. She spoke many languages and was an expert at riding horses. Jack and Jackie fell in love. They were married on September 12, 1953.

Jack's back problems had gotten worse. He was in

a lot of pain and needed crutches to walk. Not long after having an operation on his back, Jack fell into a coma and nearly died. Slowly, Jack got better, but it was months before his back healed.

During this time, Jack wrote a book about eight U.S. senators he admired. *Profiles in Courage* was published when Jack was thirty-eight. It won the Pulitzer Prize, a top prize for writers.

People admired the Kennedys for their intelligence, good looks, wit, and charm.

In 1957, Jack and Jackie had their first child, Caroline. Three years later, in 1960, John Jr. (who was called "John-John") was born.

Jack wanted to win the 1960 election for president of the United States. He was running against Richard Nixon. Was Jack too young to be president? For the first time in history, television helped voters make up their minds. Millions of people could watch Jack Kennedy and Richard Nixon on TV, talking about important topics. Jack looked calm and handsome on television. But Nixon seemed pale and nervous, and he sweated a lot.

The race was close, but Jack was voted in as the country's 35th president. At forty-three, he became the youngest man, and the first Catholic, ever elected president.

When Jack was sworn in on January 21, 1961,

he told Americans they should work to make their country better. "Ask not what your country can do for you," he said. "Ask what you can do for your country."

So many Americans loved the Kennedys. Newspapers and magazines were filled with pictures of the family. Women all

By 1960, many Americans owned television sets.

over the world copied Jackie's clothing and hairstyle. Jackie often invited famous artists, musicians, poets, and actors to the White House. The Kennedys' lives seemed fun and exciting.

Jack wanted the United States to help other countries with their problems. He started a group

Caroline liked to ride her horse, Macaroni,
on the White House lawn. John-John played
hide-and-seek under his dad's desk.

called the Peace Corps, which sends Americans to work with people in poor countries.

Before long, Jack faced trouble with the country of Cuba. Many American lawmakers did not like the way Cuba's leader, Fidel Castro, was running Cuba. Some Cubans had run away to America. Jack sent a secret force of these Cubans as soldiers to get rid of Castro. Jack was very upset when the plan—called the Bay of Pigs—failed, but he was honest about it. He told Americans that it was his fault.

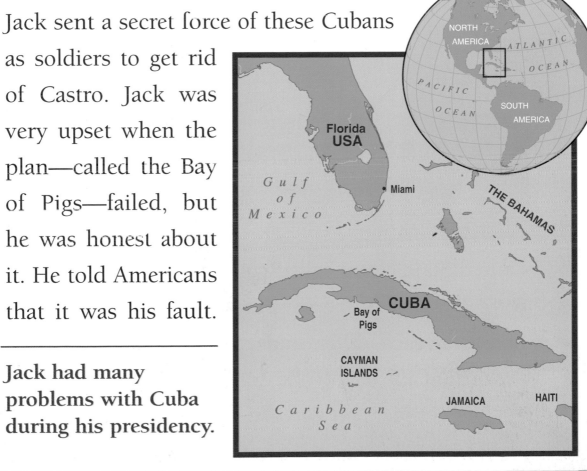

Jack had many problems with Cuba during his presidency.

Chapter 5

Tragic End

In the 1960s, the Soviet Union was the biggest country in the world. It included Russia and parts of Europe and Asia. The Soviet Union and the United States were called superpowers because they were the two strongest countries. Their leaders did not trust each other, and each country wanted to prove that its way of life was the best.

The conflict between the superpowers was called

the Cold War. It was not a "hot war"—that is, a battle with soldiers and weapons.

Both countries wanted to be the first to explore outer space. The race was on: In 1957 the Soviets launched *Sputnik*, the first satellite to orbit the earth. In 1961 the Soviets sent an astronaut into space. Just a few weeks later, Alan Shepard became the first American astronaut in space. Then, in 1962,

These are the countries that used to make up the Soviet Union.

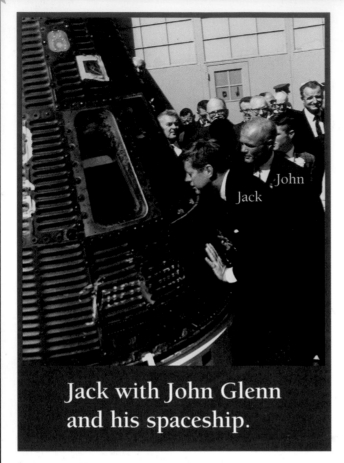

Jack with John Glenn
and his spaceship.

American astronaut John Glenn circled the earth three times. One day an American would be the first man on the moon, promised Jack.

As president, Jack wanted to do something about the unfair way that African-American men and women were treated. In the South, black children were not allowed to go to school with whites. Black people could not eat at the same restaurants or watch a movie or a ball game with whites. In October 1962, James Meredith, a black man, wanted to be a student at the University of Mississippi. Even the governor of Mississippi tried to stop him. Jack ordered soldiers to stand guard and let James sign up for classes. Later, Jack made plans for new laws to give equal rights to African Americans. He told Americans that the time had come to be fair to all people.

Blacks and whites could not even use the same water fountains.

Jack was about to face the hardest challenge of his presidency. The Soviets were setting up weapons in Cuba. It was just ninety miles from the United States. Were they planning to attack?

Jack demanded that the Soviets remove their weapons—but they did not. People in America were scared. Would the Cold War turn into a battle with airplanes carrying bombs? For two long weeks, Jack worked hard to end the crisis, called the Cuban Missile Crisis. In schools, children practiced ducking under their desks in case America was attacked. At last, on October 28, 1962, the Soviets gave in to Jack's demand. They removed their weapons from Cuba.

In 1963, Jack made a speech about the need for peace all around the world. He said he wanted "the kind of peace that makes life on earth worth living . . . not merely peace for Americans but peace for all men and women."

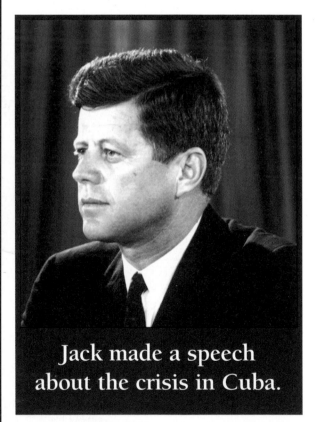

Jack made a speech about the crisis in Cuba.

Jack had many more dreams for a better world. He hoped to be elected president for another term of four years.

On November 22, 1963,

Jack traveled to Dallas, Texas, to talk to people and win more votes. As he and Jackie rode through Dallas in an open car, the sharp crack of gunshots suddenly rang out. Bullets struck Jack in the head. By the time he reached the hospital, the president was dead. A man named Lee Harvey Oswald was arrested as the killer.

The Kennedys arrived in Dallas.

Some people think Oswald liked Castro and was angry with Jack. Others think Oswald had help planning the murder. No one knows for sure. Another killer, Jack Ruby, shot Oswald the next day.

Jack's death shocked the country. People felt as if they had lost more than their beloved president. They felt they had lost hope for the future. Jack was buried

Jack's funeral was a very sad time in American history.

at Arlington National Cemetery in Virginia on November 25, 1963. During his too short time in office, Jack looked for ways to make life better for all Americans. There is a flame at his grave that reminds visitors of a special president who had many ideas for improving people's lives. John F. Kennedy brightened the spirits of the nation. He had the youth, energy, and courage to imagine an even greater country.

The flame that burns over Jack's grave will never go out.

Timeline

1917~John Fitzgerald Kennedy is born on May 29 in Brookline, Massachusetts.

1940~Graduates from Harvard University in Cambridge, Massachusetts. His book *Why England Slept* is published.

1941–1945~Serves in the U.S. Navy.

1946–1953~Is a U.S. congressman.

1953~Marries Jacqueline Bouvier on September 12.

1953–1961~Is a U.S. senator.

1957~His book *Profiles in Courage* wins the Pulitzer Prize.

1961~Becomes president after winning the election on November 8, 1960.

1963~Is shot to death on November 22.

Words to Know

boarding school—A school where students live during the school year.

missile—A weapon that is shot at a target.

politics—The workings of government.

Soviet Union (1922–1991)—A huge, powerful country made up of fifteen territories, including Russia. In 1991, the Soviet Union was divided into many separate countries.

torpedo—A weapon like a giant bullet that is fired underwater to destroy ships.

U.S. Congress—The lawmaking branch of the government. It has two parts: Senators work in the Senate, and congressmen work in the House of Representatives.

World War II—A war fought in Europe, North Africa, and Asia from 1939 to 1945. The United States, Great Britain, France, and the Soviet Union defeated Germany, Italy, and Japan.

Learn More

Books

Heiligman, Deborah. *High Hopes: A Photobiography of John F. Kennedy*. Washington, D.C.: National Geographic, 2003.

Milton, Joyce. *John F. Kennedy*. New York: DK Publishing, 2003.

Sutcliffe, Jane. *John F. Kennedy*. New York: Barnes and Noble Books, 2005.

Internet Addresses

John Fitzgerald Kennedy (1961–1963) <http://www.americanpresident.org/history/johnfkennedy/>

Biography of John F. Kennedy <http://www.whitehouse.gov/history/presidents/jk35.html>

John F. Kennedy in World War II, with photos <http://www.nationalgeographic.com/pt109/>

Index